The Case Of The
Jingle Bell Jinx

Look for more great books in

series:

⚡ The New Adventures of ⚡
MARY-KATE & ASHLEY ™

The Case Of The
Jingle Bell Jinx

by Alice Leonhardt

🍫 HarperEntertainment
An Imprint of HarperCollins*Publishers*

A PARACHUTE PRESS BOOK

PARACHUTE PRESS

Parachute Publishing, L.L.C.
156 Fifth Avenue
New York, NY 10010

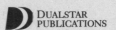
DUALSTAR PUBLICATIONS

Dualstar Publications
c/o Thorne and Company
A Professional Law Corporation
1801 Century Park East
Los Angeles, CA 90067

HarperEntertainment

An Imprint of HarperCollins*Publishers*
10 East 53rd Street, New York, NY 10022

mary-kateandashley.com
America Online Keyword: mary-kateandashley

10 9 8 7 6 5 4 3 2 1

A WINTER WONDERLAND

"**M**ary-Kate? Can you find them?" Ashley asked.

"I'm looking," I said as I rummaged through my suitcase. Where did I put those special skating passes?

My twin sister and I were at the Winter Wonderful Resort. We were on a vacation with our family.

Ashley and I were headed for the skating arena to watch our favorite figure skaters, Lisa and Terri Chan. They were practicing

for their new skating show, *Jingle Bells on Ice.*

Lisa and Terri were sisters. That was one reason Ashley and I liked them. But we could never agree on which sister we liked the best!

Ashley liked Terri because she was smooth and graceful on the ice. I liked Lisa because her jumps were always super high.

We couldn't believe it when we found out that the famous Chan sisters were practicing at *our* resort!

Now if only I could find those passes.

Ashley groaned. "I knew we should have kept them in my suitcase."

Ashley was right. She never would have lost the passes. Her clothes are packed in ABC order. Mine are packed under M, for messy.

"Ah-ha!" I held up the two passes. "Right under my nightie, where I put them."

Ashley rolled her eyes. She took the

passes and put them in her fanny pack. "For safekeeping," she told me.

We said good-bye to Mom and Dad. Then we put on our ski jackets. We walked to the arena, the snow crunching under our boots.

"Do you think we can get Terri's and Lisa's autographs?" I asked.

"They'll be too busy practicing," Ashley said. "The show is on Friday. That's just five days from now."

Lucky for us, our parents had gotten tickets for the *Jingle Bells on Ice* show. So we'd be able to see the real show, too.

We stepped inside the huge arena. It was so cold we kept our jackets on. We walked past the stands and caught our first glimpse of the skating rink.

"Wow!" I gasped. The rink was the size of a football field! A few skaters whizzed by, practicing leaps and spins.

At one end of the rink stood a ginger-bread castle. It was decorated with huge

candy canes and gumdrops.

"Cool!" Ashley exclaimed.

A woman approached us. "Are you the Trenchcoat Twins?" she asked.

"That's us," we answered together.

Ashley and I run the Olsen and Olsen Detective Agency, so a lot of people know who we are. Our office is in the attic of our house. Clue, our basset hound, usually helps us investigate crimes. But Clue stayed home this vacation.

The woman held a clipboard in one hand. Tucked under one arm was a folder full of paper.

"Pleased to meet you." She held out her free hand. "I'm Regina Filbert, the director of *Jingle Bells on Ice*. Welcome to our rehearsal. I'm very glad you're here." She sounded worried.

"Is something wrong?" Ashley asked.

"Yes. *Everything* seems to be going wrong today!" Regina answered.

I started to ask Regina what she meant. Then, out of the corner of my eye, I spotted a boy about my age. He was walking toward us with a video camera on his shoulder. And it looked as if he were filming.

"Hey! Are you guys the famous Trenchcoat Twins?" he asked.

I smiled into the camera. "That's right. Olsen and Olsen at your service."

"This is Kenny Miles." Regina introduced us. "Kenny has a special pass, too. He's filming the rehearsals and the show."

"I use the film clips for my Inside Skating Web site," Kenny explained.

"We love that Web site!" I said.

"Yeah. It has all the latest news about our favorite skaters," Ashley added.

Kenny beamed. "You should check the site out tonight. It's getting *really* interesting these days."

He swung his camera toward the opposite end of the rink. "Cool! There's Valerie

Sheffer. I've got to talk to her." He hurried off, still filming.

"Where are my skates? Has anyone seen my skates?" a girl's voice rang out.

I turned and saw the girl rush into the arena. Her short, shiny black hair bounced as she ran. She wore skater's warm-ups and a worried expression.

"Wow, it's Lisa Chan," I whispered to Ashley.

A woman followed behind Lisa. "Calm down, dear. We'll find your skates," the woman said.

Lisa whirled around to face the woman. "We won't find them, Mother. Because someone *stole* them."

"What does it matter? You have other pairs of skates," her mother pointed out.

"But I want my old ones!" Lisa wailed.

Ashley and I stared. "Why would a famous skater act like that?" I asked in a low voice.

"Maybe she's famous for her temper tantrums," Ashley whispered back.

"*Motherrr*!" a shrill cry echoed through the arena. Another girl came running around the side of the rink. She was a little bit taller than Lisa, and her black hair was cut in long layers.

"My lucky necklace is gone!" the girl cried. "Someone stole it! I can't skate without it!"

Regina bit her lip. "That's Lisa's older sister, Terri."

Ashley and I nodded. We recognized Terri right away. We had posters of her *and* her sister on our bedroom walls.

But in the posters Lisa and Terri were skating, not yelling.

Terri and Lisa ran toward Regina. Their mother followed behind.

"Regina! You're the director! Round up a search party!" Terri said. "We need to find my lucky—"

"No, we need to find my skates first!" Lisa cut in. "I don't want to miss my ice time."

"Girls, calm down!" Regina held up her hand. "You're in luck. These are the Trenchcoat Twins, Ashley and Mary-Kate Olsen."

"The Trenchcoat Twins!" Lisa exclaimed. "Super! Can you find my skates?"

"Can you find my necklace, too?" Terri asked.

Ashley and I smiled at each other. It looked like we had a new case on our hands.

"We'll do our best," Ashley and I promised.

"Thank you!" Lisa smiled brightly.

"Thank you *very much*!" Terri gave us an even brighter smile.

Ashley grabbed her notebook and pencil from her fanny pack. "We need to ask you some questions. Do you know who might have taken your lucky necklace?" she asked Terri.

"And do you have any idea who might have taken your skates?" I asked Lisa.

Terri and Lisa glared at each other.

They pointed fingers at each other.

"*She did it!*" they hollered at the same time.

TROUBLE TIMES TWO

For a second, I stood there with my mouth hanging open. I couldn't believe it! The sisters were accusing *each other*?

"Wait a minute," Ashley said. "Terri, are you saying that Lisa took your necklace?"

Terri nodded. "Our dressing room stays locked. No one else could get in there."

"That's right." Lisa made a smug face. "Which means Terri is the only one who could have taken my skates!"

"Why do you think Terri would steal

your necklace, Lisa?" I asked.

"Terri will do *anything* to be the Ice Princess," Lisa said. "She knows I need my old skates to skate my best."

"It's Lisa who will do *anything* to be the Ice Princess," Terri snapped. "My necklace helps *me* skate my best."

Ashley closed her notebook. "We'll check it out," she told the sisters. "Meanwhile, just go ahead with your practice."

The two sisters took off, still arguing, with their mother trailing behind them. Regina sighed. "The girls keep arguing over who is going to be Ice Princess!" she said. "It's ruining practice."

"Who's the Ice Princess?" Ashley asked.

"The 'star' of the show," Regina explained. "The Ice Princess has a solo."

"Why are you choosing her so late?" I asked.

"We have three very strong skaters here, Terri and Lisa, of course, plus Valerie

Sheffer," Regina told us. "We wanted to see who was skating her best before we assigned the solo."

Valerie was an amazing skater. Two years ago, Ashley and I watched her on TV when she competed in the Olympics.

"How will you choose the Ice Princess?" Ashley asked.

Regina tapped her clipboard. "Patrick and I are keeping notes on who is skating the best during practice."

"Who is Patrick?" I asked.

Regina pointed to the ice. A young man with shaggy blond hair stood there talking to three skaters. "He's the show's choreographer. He designed the skating routines and created the Ice Princess solo."

Lisa hurried up to us. A pair of skates was hanging from her shoulder.

"Oh good, you found your skates," Regina said.

"No, these are *new* skates," Lisa complained as she put them on. "They hurt my feet."

I sat next to her. "Don't worry," I said. "My sister and I will help you find your skates."

"Thanks!" Lisa said. With a wave, she glided onto the ice.

"We need to help Terri, too," Ashley reminded me.

"You'll be helping both of them." Regina smiled. "And the show!"

Regina walked away. We sat down in the stands to watch Lisa. She had the ice all to herself. She started her routine with a tremendous jump. Then she spun in a circle so quickly, it made me dizzy to watch her.

I sighed. "I wish we could skate like that."

Ashley and I had taken skating lessons when we were little. My fanciest move was falling on my face.

"You'd have to practice at least six hours every day," someone behind us said.

We turned around to find Kenny stand-

ing there. "That's how much Lisa and Terri practice," he finished.

"How do you know?" Ashley asked.

"I've been here all week covering the show," Kenny bragged.

"Do you know about the weird stuff happening around here?" Ashley asked him.

Kenny nodded. "It's making a great story for my Web site." He grinned at us. "I'm calling it The Jingle Bell Jinx."

"Catchy," I said.

"No, no!" Loud yelling came from the rink. Ashley and I turned around to see what was going on.

Kenny pointed to the man who was yelling. "That's Valerie's coach, Jake Biggs," he said.

"The triple highfly has three rotations!" Jake shouted at Valerie. "Try it again!"

Kenny whipped his large camera to his shoulder and started filming. "Excellent! More juicy stuff for the Web site."

Valerie glided across the ice. She leaped up and tried to spin three times in the air. But after only two rotations, she landed awkwardly on the ice.

"What's a triple highfly?" I asked Kenny.

"It's some tricky new move Jake created," Kenny said. "But Valerie can't do it."

"All right. Let's quit for now," we heard Jake say. He sounded frustrated.

"I've got to get my laptop computer and add this stuff to the Web site," Kenny told us. "See you guys later."

"Later," Ashley and I called. Kenny sped down the bleachers.

"He really does know a lot about what's going on," Ashley said.

"Yeah," I agreed. "Maybe he can help us figure out why all this bad stuff is happening to Lisa and Terri."

Jake and Valerie passed in front of us as they came off the ice. Ashley and I pretended to be busy watching Lisa. But we were

listening to Jake and Valerie's conversation.

"Don't worry," Jake said to Valerie. "Tomorrow you'll nail that third spin."

"I hope so." Valerie sighed. "Regina has to pick *me* to be Ice Princess."

Jake patted her shoulder. "Stick with me, Val. And you'll be the star. I guarantee it!"

They pushed through a door labeled LOCKER ROOMS.

Ashley turned to me. "Wow! It sounds like Valerie really wants to be the Ice Princess."

"Enough to steal Terri's lucky necklace?" I asked.

"And Lisa's skates," Ashley added. She pulled out her notepad. I peeked over her shoulder. She wrote: *Possible suspect: Valerie Sheffer.*

"Come on, Ashley." I jumped up from my seat. "Let's go talk to Valerie and see what we can find out!"

As Ashley stood up, the lights suddenly

went out! The arena was plunged into total darkness.

Ashley gasped.

I stumbled.

And a girl on the ice let out a terrifying scream. "Help me! Oh, no. Somebody help me!"

IN THE DARK

The girl screamed again.

"That's Lisa!" I cried. "She was practicing when the lights went out."

I turned to the rink. "Stay where you are, Lisa!" I hollered.

Click. The overhead emergency lights flickered on. They cast a dim yellow glow over the arena. Ashley reached into her fanny pack for her flashlight and switched it on.

Holding on to each other, Ashley and I

made our way down the bleachers and stepped on the ice.

"Whoa!" I shouted as my feet almost slid out from under me.

We aimed the flashlight toward Lisa. She lay sprawled on the ice. She clutched her right knee. Tears streamed down her face.

We helped Lisa stand and guided her off the ice.

"Thank you!" She sat down on a bench and rubbed her knee. "It's okay." She sighed with relief.

Terri came running toward us. She carried a flashlight of her own. "What happened?" she asked.

"You know what happened!" Lisa exclaimed. "*You* turned off the lights. So I'd fall!"

Terri's mouth dropped open. "Me? No way! I was in the dressing room looking for my necklace."

The arena lights came on full force. I

squinted as my eyes adjusted to the bright light.

I spotted Valerie standing on the other side of the rink. She stared at us. Then she turned and disappeared through an exit.

Very suspicious, I thought.

"Where were you when the lights went out?" Kenny charged up to us. He was panting for breath as he pointed his camera at Lisa.

Lisa blocked the camera with her hand. "I was on the ice, Mr. Nosy!"

Ashley gave me a nudge. "We need to figure out why the lights went out," she whispered. "Let's do some investigating."

"Good idea," I said. "Let's find out where the light switches are."

We headed for the same set of doors Valerie had gone through. They were the doors that led to the locker rooms.

"LADIES' LOCKER ROOM, MEN'S LOCKER ROOM..." I read the signs as we walked down the hall.

Ashley stopped in front of a door that had two stars on it. Terri's name was written in one star. Lisa's in the other. "This must be the Chan sisters' dressing room," she said.

At the end of the hall I spotted a bald man wearing a navy blue maintenance uniform. He was coming out of a door ahead of us labeled DANGER, HIGH VOLTAGE.

"The electrical room!" I exclaimed. "The lights must be controlled from in there!"

Ashley and I hurried over to the man.

"Excuse me, sir," Ashley said. "Can you tell us what happened to the lights?"

"Don't worry, girls." The man smiled. "I just had a look. Someone shut off the main light switch. But I turned it back on."

"Did you see anything suspicious in the room?" Ashley asked.

"Nope." He scratched his bald head. "I didn't really look." He turned back to the electrical room. "I'd better check it out."

We followed the man into the room. It was filled with switches and wires.

"Here's the main control for the lights," he said. He pointed to a big switch.

"And here's a clue!" I whispered. On the floor I spotted a fuzzy blue tassel—the kind skaters wear on their laces. I picked it up. Then Ashley and I left the room.

Ashley grinned. "Now we just have to find the matching tassel!"

"Where should we start?" I asked. "There are tons of skaters in this show. Any one of them could have the match."

"Let's start with Valerie," Ashley said. "*She* has the best motive for trying to hurt Lisa."

"*And* she was close to the electrical room," I remembered. "When the lights went back on, she was standing right outside the locker room doors."

We walked down the hall and entered the ladies' locker room. Valerie was changing out of her warm-up clothes. I tried to see her skates, but they were hidden behind her skating bag.

"So, Valerie, what do you think of all the weird things happening to the Chan sisters?" Ashley asked.

Valerie gave us a suspicious look. "Who are you?"

"We're Mary-Kate and Ashley Olsen. We're detectives," I explained. "Regina asked us to look into things. She wants the show to go smoothly."

Valerie snorted. "Then she should throw Lisa and Terri out. Their arguing is getting on everybody's nerves!"

"And if they were gone, *you* would get to be the Ice Princess, right?" Ashley asked.

"I don't need to get rid of Terri and Lisa," Valerie said smugly. "They're skating so badly, they'll never get picked to be the Ice Princess. I'm going to beat them fair and square."

She picked up her skates and shoved them into her bag. I glanced at the laces.

No blue tassel.

With a wave of her fingers, Valerie walked out of the locker room.

We headed back to the rink where the song "Winter Wonderland" was playing over the sound system. Above the cheerful music Patrick, the choreographer, was hollering, "Leap, spin, glide!"

On the ice, Terri and five other girls were dressed as snowflakes. Patrick directed everyone.

Ashley and I sat in the stands to watch.

I squinted to see the girls' skates. But the skaters were too far away for me to notice if anyone had a blue tassel on their laces.

Ashley smiled dreamily. "Wow, Terri's an awesome skater."

Boom. Boom. Boom. The sound of a bass drum filled the arena, interrupting "Winter Wonderland."

"What's that?" Ashley asked.

Boom. Ba-da boom. It was a rap song. And it was blasting from the sound system.

I plugged my ears.

On the rink, the skating snowflakes stopped in confusion. Terri was in the middle of a triple toe loop.

"You're never gonna get it," the rap group sang. "So don't you fret it. 'Cause I'm going to be the star!"

Terri turned in surprise. She missed her landing and fell to the ice. With a cry of pain, she clutched her ankle.

Ashley and I jumped up from our seats.

"Oh, no!" Ashley cried. "Now Terri's hurt!"

Ashley and I rushed onto the ice. Slipping and sliding, we made our way to Terri. The snowflake skaters gathered around her.

"How could Lisa do this to me?" Terri wailed.

"Lisa? What makes you think she did this?" I asked.

"'Wanna Be a Star' is her favorite song!" Terri told us.

Regina ran up to us with an ice pack in her hand. "Sit still a minute, Terri."

"No, I've got to practice." Terri tried to stand. She wobbled on one skate.

I glanced down at her feet. Terri was wearing a blue tassel on her left skate!

4

A SLIPPERY SITUATION

"**W**here is the sound booth?" Ashley asked Regina.

Regina pointed to a ramp on the left side of the rink. It led upward to a walkway around the top tier of the stands.

"Quick!" Ashley said. "Let's go! Maybe we can catch the music-switcher in the act!"

"Wait—take a look Terri's skate," I whispered.

Ashley stopped in her tracks. "A blue tassel! It looks like the exact match to the

one we found in the electrical room!"

"This is crazy!" I said. "Can one sister really be sabotaging the other? Sisters are supposed to stick together. Like us! They're not supposed to try to hurt each other!"

"I know," Ashley said. "Well, let's check out the sound booth for clues."

I followed Ashley across the ice and up the steep ramp to the sound booth.

I threw open the door and saw—Kenny and Mrs. Chan?

"What are you guys doing in here?" I asked.

"Mrs. Chan asked me to help," Kenny explained. "We ran to check out the booth."

"Who is doing these awful things to my girls?" Mrs. Chan looked ready to cry.

"No one was here when we came in, but we found this." Kenny held up a tape. "Wanna Be a Star" was written on the label. "I can't find 'Winter Wonderland' anywhere."

Ashley sighed. "Whoever switched the

tapes must have taken 'Winter Wonderland' with them."

I showed Mrs. Chan the "Wanna Be a Star" tape. "Does this look like Lisa's handwriting?"

"It could be. But Lisa didn't switch the music," she added quickly. "The girls would never do anything like this to each other."

She twisted her hands together. "I'd better see if Terri's all right."

"I'm going with you," Kenny said to Mrs. Chan. "Maybe I can interview her for the Web site."

When the two of them left, I turned to Ashley. "Let's find Lisa and ask her about this tape."

We headed down the ramp to the rink. Then we hurried to the locker rooms.

Ashley knocked hard on Terri and Lisa's dressing room door. It was unlocked. Slowly, it swung open.

"Is...is anyone in here?" I called. No one answered.

"I thought they said they kept their dressing room locked," Ashley whispered.

We glanced around the room. It had two dressing tables and a closet. But Terry and Lisa's stuff was thrown all over the place!

I gasped. "Oh, no! Someone must have broken in!"

Lisa came into the room. "Hey, Mary-Kate. Hi, Ashley. What are you doing in here?"

"We were looking for you. But instead we found this!" I waved at the mess in the room.

Lisa smiled. "Not too neat, huh?"

Ashley and I gave each other embarrassed grins. No one had broken in. The Chan sisters were just super messy.

"Is this yours?" I asked. I held up the "Wanna Be a Star" tape. I crossed my fingers. I didn't want the tape to be Lisa's.

"Hey, that *is* mine!" Lisa answered. "Where did you get it?"

LINING UP THE SUSPECTS

Ashley squinted at Lisa. She seemed to be studying her. "Where were you fifteen minutes ago?" Ashley asked.

"In the locker room. Looking for my missing skates." Lisa frowned. "Why?"

"Because someone switched your tape with the 'Winter Wonderland' song," I said. "The switch made Terri fall."

"Well, I didn't do it," Lisa said. "Someone must have stolen my tape!"

Two hours later, Ashley and I were

standing on top of the resort's snow tubing hill. We decided to take a break from our case and have some fun!

We placed our tube down on the snow. Then we sat in the center of it. Holding on to each other, we pushed off.

"Wheeeeeaah!" we screamed as we zoomed down the hill.

"Cool!" I exclaimed when we finally hit the bottom.

"You mean cold!" Ashley's cheeks were bright red. She jumped from the tube.

Suddenly, her eyes grew wide.

"What is it?" I asked.

Ashley pointed to the right, toward the ski lift. Two kids were arguing loudly with a man wearing snow goggles.

We recognized the kids right away— Terri and Lisa!

But who was that man?

"You two girls are spoiled and undisciplined," the man said. "And your nonstop arguing is ruining the show."

"It's not my fault I fell!" Terri told him. "It's Lisa's. She switched the tapes."

"Did not!" Lisa fired back.

"Did, too!" Terri yelled.

"Quiet!" the man roared. "You should be practicing right now. Not playing in the snow."

"Oh, quit yelling at us, Jake," Terri said.

Jake? Did she mean Jake Biggs? Valerie Sheffer's coach? Why was he yelling at Terri and Lisa?

"Fine," Jake growled. "But *neither* of you will ever be the Ice Princess!"

Jake stomped off.

"Oh, great," I heard Terri say. "Now Jake's going to make sure Valerie gets to be Ice Princess."

"No way," Lisa said. "I'm getting the part."

"You? Give me one reason why Regina would give it to you," Terri demanded.

"Because you're a klutz!" Lisa shouted.

Ashley rolled her eyes at me. "There they go again," she whispered.

"We'd better break it up," I said.

After we calmed the sisters, Ashley and I returned to our room.

"Terri and Lisa sure are mad at each other," I said to Ashley.

"Well, switching songs was an awful thing for Lisa to do to Terri," Ashley said.

"But we're not sure Lisa did it," I said. "And what about Terri turning the lights out on Lisa? We found her tassel in the electrical room!"

"That doesn't prove anything," Ashley insisted. "Just like the tape in the sound booth doesn't prove Lisa switched the music."

We stared at each other for a second. Then I slumped down on my bed. "We're starting to sound just like Terri and Lisa." I groaned.

"That's because this case is totally hard!"

Ashley admitted. "We don't know if Lisa's the culprit—"

"—or if it's Terri—" I put in.

"—or if someone else is doing all these things but making it look like the sisters are doing them," Ashley finished.

"Someone like Valerie?" I wondered.

"Or Jake," Ashley guessed. "Maybe he wants the Chans out of the show so Valerie will get to be Ice Princess."

"We need to add Jake to our list of suspects," I told her.

We both sighed. Too many suspects. What a crazy case!

"You know what else we need to do?" I jumped up from the bed. "We need to check out Kenny's Web site. Maybe it will help us narrow down the suspects."

"Good idea," Ashley agreed. "And you know what's another good idea?"

"What?" I asked.

Ashley gave me a big grin. "Hot chocolate!"

• • •

Minutes later we were settled in front of a roaring fire with some hot chocolate and our dad's laptop.

"Keep your fingers crossed that something on the Web site will help us," Ashley said. She opened the Inside Skating Web site.

The first page had a photo of the two Chan sisters. They wore medals around their necks. They were waving and smiling.

"It will be nice to solve this case," I said. "So Terri and Lisa can stop fighting."

Ashley moved the mouse. She clicked on an article called "The Jingle Bell Jinx."

We read it silently. "No new clues there," I said. "It's just a summary of the stuff that's been happening at the show."

Ashley moved the mouse to another link. "Sisters Fire Skating Coach."

"I wonder what *this* is about?" she said. She clicked on the article.

I read the title aloud. "Terri and Lisa

Chan Fire Coach Jake Biggs."

"Jake used to be Terri and Lisa's coach?" Ashley asked.

"According to this article," I said. "The girls fired him a month ago. They said he was too strict."

"Maybe Jake should be suspect number one," Ashley said. "He has two reasons to make the sisters look bad."

"That's right. He wants Valerie to win," I said.

"*And* he's probably mad at Terri and Lisa for firing him!" Ashley added.

"Okay. Coach Biggs is our number one suspect," I said. "Tomorrow let's spy on him. We'll see if he does anything suspicious."

"But how can we spy on him?" Ashley asked. "Jake's already seen us around the rink. He knows who we are!"

I grinned. "Don't worry. I have a plan!"

6

BREAKING IN

The next morning, Regina, Ashley, and I stood in the *Jingle Bells on Ice* wardrobe room. "No one will know who you are in those outfits," Regina said. "They're the perfect disguises!"

Ashley and I waddled over to the mirror. We were wearing big foam costumes.

Ashley was a candy cane. She had a tall red and white hook-shaped head and a long, skinny body.

I was a gingerbread man. I had a big fat

cookie-shaped head and a large, flat body. Regina put makeup on us, too. Ashley had a red-and-white striped face. I had a brown-dotted one.

Jake would never recognize us in these getups. I hardly recognized myself!

Regina handed us skates. "I think these are the right size. They're extras."

"Thanks." We sat down to put them on. Then we carefully stood up together. I tried to take a step forward—and crashed into Ashley!

"Uhh...we're not exactly the greatest skaters," Ashley explained to Regina.

Holding on to each other, Ashley and I wobbled up to the rink. A dozen other skaters—all dressed like candies or cookies—were there warming up.

"Do you see Jake anywhere?" I whispered to Ashley.

"No. Not yet," Ashley answered.

"Hey, you two!" someone shouted.

Ashley and I looked around.

Patrick was waving at us from the rink. "Yo! Candy cane and gingerbread girl! Over here!"

"Umm…us?" I asked.

"Yes, you. You're late! Get on the ice with the others," Patrick ordered. "We're working on a few changes."

"But—but—," Ashley stammered.

"Just go along with it! We don't want to blow our cover!" I whispered in her ear.

We pulled off our skate guards. Together, we glided gracefully onto the ice—sort of. We took our place behind a row of gumdrops.

"When the song starts, we do a waltz jump, then a single loop," Patrick said. He demonstrated the combination.

I gulped. I had never done either of those moves before!

Help! I thought. *Regina, get us out of here!*

I searched the sidelines for her, and

spotted—Jake! He was pacing around the arena.

He stopped at an exit. He checked behind him—as if to make sure no one was watching. Then he disappeared through the doors that led to the locker rooms.

"Ashley!" I called, keeping my voice voice low. "It's Jake! We've got to follow him."

"We can't follow him now!" Ashley whispered back. "We're supposed to be skating sweets!"

"One, two, three." Patrick clapped as he counted. "Begin!"

The music started. It was a song about yummy treats, but I couldn't pay attention to the words. I was too busy trying not to fall!

"Leap!" Patrick called. We all leaped.

"Yikes!" Ashley yelped. She nearly wiped out on her landing.

"Now spin!" Patrick ordered.

"Whoooooa!" As I spun my body, my head became dizzy. And I twirled right into Ashley!

I linked my arm with hers, and the two of us began spinning around and around.

"Oof!" We stopped ourselves by crashing into the side of the rink.

"Hey! Where are you two going!" Patrick hollered.

"Wardrobe," I called, my head still swimming. "I ripped my costume!"

Ashley grinned as we hopped off the ice. "Quick thinking, Mary-Kate."

Arms still linked, I led Ashley around the rink and through the doors that led to the locker room.

We walked down the hall, then peeked around the corner. Jake was standing in front of Terri and Lisa's dressing room door.

I turned to Ashley. Her candy cane head poked me in my nose. "Ow!" I cried. "Watch where you put that thing."

"Sorry," Ashley apologized. "It's hard to lay low when you're dressed like a five-foot dessert." She stood on her tiptoes trying to peek around the corner. "What's he doing?" she asked in a low voice.

"He's standing in front of the dressing room door," I reported. I peeked around the corner again. "He's pulling out a screwdriver."

"A screwdriver?" Ashley peered over my shoulder. Jake poked the end of the screwdriver into the doorknob. He rattled the knob. Then he opened the door and slipped inside.

"He broke into their dressing room!" I gasped.

"I bet I know why," Ashley said. "He's stealing something of Terri's. Like that tassel. Then he'll use it to make her look guilty."

"Or he's stealing something of Lisa's," I said. "Like her rap tape. Then he'll use it to make *her* look guilty."

"Let's catch him in the act." Ashley pushed past me. Her blade caught on my gingerbread foot. I grabbed her just before she fell.

We shuffled to the door. It was open a crack. Ashley threw the door wide and shouted, "Caught you!"

Surprised, Jake jumped in the air. "What do you mean?" He held a videocassette in his hand.

"Why are you taking that cassette?" I demanded.

"Why do you want to know?" He peered at us. "And who are you?"

I forgot—we were in disguise.

"We're detectives," Ashley said. "We're trying to find the person who's playing tricks on Terri and Lisa."

"And it looks like we caught the culprit," I added. "*You!*" I tried to sound tough, but it's hard to do when you're dressed like a cookie.

Jake held up the cassette. "Well, you caught the wrong guy. I'm not taking a cassette. I'm leaving it.'

"*Leaving* it?" Ashley sounded puzzled.

"It's a video instruction of how to perform my creation. The triple highfly," Jake said. "I want Terri and Lisa to watch it."

"Why?" Ashley asked.

Jake sighed. "Because they're the only skaters talented enough to learn it."

"What about Valerie?" I asked.

He shook his head. "Valerie tries hard. But she's not going to get it."

I narrowed my eyes at Jake. I wasn't convinced he was telling the truth. "Why would you want Lisa and Terri to perform the jump? Didn't they fire you?" I asked.

"Yes. But it was a mistake," Jake told us. "Once Lisa and Terri see my new jump, they'll hire me back. They'll perform the move, and I'll be famous!"

Ashley put her fists on her candy cane

hips. "Wait a minute. Something still doesn't add up. Why did you break into their dressing room?"

"I tried to give them this tape before," Jake said. "But they wouldn't take it. So I decided to leave it for them."

Ashley and I exchanged a glance. Was he telling the truth?

Jake handed me the tape. "Make sure the girls watch this. Tell them I want to be their coach again. Together, we can all be super famous." He turned and left the dressing room.

"Sounds like we should scratch Jake off our list of suspects," I told Ashley.

Ashley nodded. "He doesn't want Terri and Lisa to skate badly—or leave the show."

"Right. He just wants them to perform the triple highfly," I agreed.

I set Jake's videocassette on the girls' dressing table.

Ashley reached into her costume and

took out her notepad and a pencil. She scratched Coach Biggs's name off our list of suspects. I stared at the rest of the list—Valerie Shiffer, Lisa Chan, and Terry Chan.

Ashley tapped her red-and-white candy-cane lips with the end of the pencil. "Jake wants to coach Terri and Lisa," she said. "If he did that, he would have to stop coaching Valerie."

"Yeah!" I realized. "And if he dropped Valerie, she'd be furious!"

"*Super* furious," Ashley said. "Because Terri and Lisa would have stolen her coach. Then they'd perform the triple highfly—and be way more famous than she is!"

"So *Valerie* has a double motive for wanting Terri and Lisa out of the way," I said. I grinned at Ashley.

"Let's make her our new number-one suspect." Ashley wrote a big "#1" next to Valerie's name. "Come on. Let's do some detecting."

"Wait—let's take our skates off first." I bent to untie them. "It'll be easier to sneak around."

"Good idea." Ashley leaned over.

Clang! Her foam head knocked into a lamp. The lamp wobbled, but I straightened it out before it could fall.

Barefoot now, we tiptoed down the hall to the locker room. We were lucky. No one was there. And Valerie's lock was hanging open.

"Excellent!" I whispered. "What luck!"

Ashley stopped by the doorway. "You check out the locker. "I'll keep watch," she said.

I looked inside the locker door. I expected to find some really good evidence like Lisa's skates or Terri's necklace. But the only thing in it was Valerie's warm up suit. It hung from the hook.

"There's nothing here," I said, disappointed. Then I noticed something sticking out of her pants pocket—a cassette tape!

I pulled it out. "Winter Wonderland" was written on the outside. I turned to Ashley. Awesome! This was evidence. Evidence that Valerie switched the tape!

"Mary-Kate," Ashley whispered. "Somebody's coming. Hide!"

7

THE COLD CONFESSION

"There. In the showers." Ashley grabbed my arm and yanked me along with her. I closed the locker door and shoved the tape inside my costume.

Just in time, we stuffed ourselves, with our big bulky costumes, into the nearest shower stall.

Ashley put a finger to her lips. I held my breath.

"Boy, Patrick made us practice forever," someone complained.

Plop. Something wet dripped on my hand.

I glanced up. The showerhead was leaking on us!

"All because of that goofy gingerbread girl," another voice said. "And that klutzy candy cane."

Goofy? Klutzy? I thought. I felt my cheeks turn red.

Plop, plop. Two more drops fell on me. Yuck. I turned to Ashley. She was wet, too. Water was dripping right onto her head.

"Who were those kids, anyway?" the first voice asked.

"Probably friends of Regina's. That's the only way they could have gotten parts in the show."

The girls laughed, then I heard the clunk of their blades as they left the room.

Ashley and I climbed out of the shower stall.

"Ick," Ashley said. "I'm all soggy."

She was right. The red stripes on her

face had run into her white stripes. Now she was pink and drippy. Her candy cane head drooped.

"Your disguise is ruined," I told her.

She giggled. "Yours, too. You look like a gingerbread blob."

I glanced down. My costume was saggy and round instead of cookie-shaped.

"So much for our disguises," I said. "Hey, how about if we're just Mary-Kate and Ashley for a while. You know, the super detectives? Who solved the mystery?" I reached inside my costume—and pulled out the "Winter Wonderland" tape.

Ashley's mouth dropped open. "Valerie had 'Winter Wonderland!' That means she switched the tapes!"

"Looks like it," I said.

"So *she's* been playing all those tricks on Terri and Lisa."

"Right." I nodded my soggy head. "But we're going to need more evidence before we can say anything about this to anyone. Come on, we've got more work to do."

We left the locker room and headed toward the wardrobe room to change. I should have felt happy. After all, it seemed like we were about to solve the case!

Instead, I frowned. "Do you think it's strange that Valerie's locker was left open?" I asked Ashley.

"I guess it *is* strange." Ashley opened the door into the wardrobe room. "But maybe Valerie just forgot to lock it."

"Maybe." I pulled off my cookie head. "Terri and Lisa should be in the arena by now. Let's go find them and tell them about Jake's tape."

We changed into our regular clothes. It felt good to be dry again.

We found Terri, Lisa, and Mrs. Chan in Terri and Lisa's dressing room. Ashley told them what Jake had said. Terri and Lisa agreed to watch the tape.

I went to the table to get it for them, but I didn't see it anywhere.

"Uh, Ashley? It's not here," I said.

"Not here?" Ashley came over to help look. "What do you mean?"

"Hey, everybody! Want to see my new costume?" Terri asked us. "It's totally cool. It's for the Jingle Jazz routine."

She pulled a plastic covered hanger from the closet. She slid off the plastic. The costume had a short flared skirt and a scooped neck. It was covered with bright blue sequins that shimmered in the light.

"It's beautiful!" Ashley and I exclaimed.

"Oh, no! It's ruined!" Terri gasped. She pointed to the hem of the skirt. It was decorated with tiny bells. But half of the bells had been torn off!

Terri spun and faced her sister. Her face was bright red. "How could you!" she accused.

"Me?" Lisa looked shocked.

"Yes, *you*. I knew you would be jealous of my outfit. But I didn't think you'd ruin it!"

"I didn't!" Lisa insisted.

"We'll figure out who did this to your costume," Ashley said. "You two have to go and practice."

"Fine," Terri said. She glared at Lisa as they left the dressing room.

I slapped my forehead with my hand. "I can't believe this! Valerie stole the videotape and ruined Terri's costume!"

"Hold on. We can't jump to conclusions, Mary-Kate," Ashley said. "I think it's Valerie, too. But let's check around here for clues. Then we'll go talk to her."

"I'll start in the closet," I said. "That's where Terri's costume was hanging. Maybe our culprit dropped something in there."

Ashley went over to the dressing table. "I'll hunt for the cassette. Maybe no one took it. Maybe it's still around here somewhere."

I opened a skating bag. It had leg warmers in it. It also had a pair of tennis shoes and—little tiny bells. Bells that matched the ones on Terri's costume!

I gasped, totally surprised. "Wow. Check this out, Ashley. The missing bells are in this bag!"

Ashley's eyes widened. She took the bag. We noticed the name "Lisa Chan" was written on the side.

"This is *Lisa's* bag!" Ashley raised her eyebrows. I knew what she was thinking.

"No way. Lisa did not do this," I stated. "Valerie must have planted the bells in her bag. We just have to prove it."

Out of the corner of my eye, I saw something at the bottom of the closet. A tiny silver snowflake.

I showed it to Ashley. "Do either of the Chan sisters have a costume covered with snowflakes?"

Ashley and I checked the hangers. There

was an elf outfit and a lollipop costume. The blue sequined dress, and a red-and-green dress made of satin. No snowflakes anywhere.

"I bet that snowflake is Valerie's," Ashley said.

I nodded. "Let's go have a talk with her."

We hurried into the arena. Kenny was sitting in the stands, typing on his laptop. Several gumdrop skaters were on the ice working with Patrick. The gingerbread castle had been moved to the middle of the rink.

"They must be rehearsing the final number," I said to Ashley.

Ashley pointed across the ice. "There's Valerie! She's stretching out next to the rink. And she's wearing a *snowflake-covered* costume!"

Ashley and I ran over to her. I looked closely at her costume.

"There!" Ashley pointed at Valerie's skirt. A snowflake was missing from it!

"*There* what?" Valerie asked.

I held up the snowflake we found in the Chan sisters' dressing room. "I'm sorry. Does this belong to you?" I asked Valerie.

"Yes," Valerie said. "Where did you find it?"

"In Terri and Lisa's dressing room," I said.

Valerie looked scared. Then she broke down. "All right. You caught me!" she cried.

8

RUNNING OUT OF TIME

Ashley and I grinned at each other. Another case solved by the Trenchcoat Twins!

"We thought it was you," Ashley said. "That means you stole Terri's necklace."

"And Lisa's skates," I added. "And you shut the lights when she was practicing!"

Valerie stared at us as if we were crazy. "What are you talking about? I didn't do those things!"

"Of course you did," I explained. "So you

could get the part of the Ice Princess."

"I don't need to play tricks on the Chans to be the Ice Princess," Valerie said. "They skated so badly that yesterday Regina made *me* Ice Princess."

"She did?" Mary-Kate and I exclaimed.

Valerie nodded. "She's telling Terri and Lisa about it before rehearsal." She glanced down at the floor. "But I did do one thing wrong. I went into Terri and Lisa's dressing room and took Jake's videotape."

"Why?" Ashley asked.

Valerie sniffed loudly. "I heard him say that he wanted Terri and Lisa to perform the triple highfly, because I'm not good enough!" She wiped away a tear.

Ashley pulled a tissue from her fanny pack. She handed it to Valerie.

"So you *didn't* play all those tricks on Terri and Lisa?" I asked.

She shook her head. "I've been in competitions since I was five years old. I don't

DETECTIVE TRICK

CIRCLE CODE

Run rings around your enemies with this fun code.

Draw a circle like the one below. Write your message one letter at a time in every other space on the circle. Put an arrow where your message starts. For example, if your message is "jingle bells" your wheel would look like this:

To crack the code, tell your friend to start at the arrow and write out every other letter in a clockwise direction on a piece of paper. When he or she is done, your message will be clear!

mary-kateandashley.com
America Online Keyword: mary-kateandashley

From
The Case Of The JINGLE BELL JINX

DETECTIVE TRICK

COMPUTER GAMES

Send a hidden message to your friend by computer! Here's how: Type the message to your friend. Then take the following steps to make the text disappear:

1. Highlight the text.
2. Change the color of the text to white. You can do this by choosing Format, then Font, and then Color.
3. Attach the word file to an E-mail—then send it to your friend!

When he or she receives the E-mail, all he/she has to do is highlight the blank page, change the font color back to black, and read your message!

mary-kateandashley.com
America Online Keyword: mary-kateandashley

Look for our next mystery…
The Case Of The GAME SHOW MYSTERY

play tricks, and I've never cheated."

"Then what about this?" I asked. I held up the "Winter Wonderland" tape.

"What's that?" Valerie asked.

"It's Terri's missing tape," Ashley explained. "We found it in your locker."

Valerie blew her nose. "Wait a minute. How did you guys get into my locker?"

"Your lock was left open," Ashley said.

Valerie seemed surprised. "No way! I always keep it locked."

"Which means someone else might have left it open," Ashley said. "Someone who wanted to make Valerie look guilty!"

"Valerie! It's your skate time!" Jake waved from the ice.

Valerie sighed. "I've got to go. I need to tell Jake that I know he doesn't want to be my coach anymore."

I patted her shoulder again. "At least you're the Ice Princess!"

Her face brightened. "Yes, I am. And I'll

be the best Ice Princess ever."

When she skated off, Ashley looked at me. "Oh, boy. We sure made a mistake."

"Where did we go wrong?" I shook my head. "All the evidence pointed to Valerie."

Someone chuckled behind us. We whirled around—and saw Kenny! His video camera was aimed at us. He had taped our whole conversation with Valerie!

Kenny swung the camera off his shoulder. "With all this juicy stuff going on, my Web site's going to get a ton of hits tomorrow!"

We heard arguing from the sidelines. Regina was talking to Terri and Lisa.

"I've had enough of your fighting," Regina said. "If you girls don't stop your bickering and start skating well, I'm taking you out of the show completely!"

I clutched Ashley's shoulder.

Our favorite skaters not in the show? No way! Ashley and I had to solve this case— fast!

9

A SHOCKING DISCOVERY

Kenny turned his camera on the scene. I blocked the lens with my hand. "Kenny, quit taping. This is private stuff."

"Okay." He flushed red with embarrassment. "I'll go get a quote from Jake." He hurried off.

When Kenny left, Ashley turned to me. "Mary-Kate, time's running out. We have to figure out who else would want the sisters out of the show."

I frowned. "I know! And if we cross Lisa

and Terry off of our suspect list, there's no one left!"

"I feel like we're missing some big fat clue," Ashley said.

"Let's take another look at Kenny's Web site," I suggested. "Maybe we missed something."

We checked around for Kenny. I didn't see him anywhere. I spotted his laptop on a seat in the stands. "Do you think he would mind if we used his computer?"

"No. He's always excited when his site gets another hit," Ashley pointed out.

Ashley sat down and placed Kenny's laptop on her lap. The computer was already on. "Looks like Kenny was writing something," she said.

She peered at the screen. Her eyes widened. "Mary-Kate!" She gasped. "You've got to read this!"

THE SHOW GOES ON

I leaned closer to read the computer screen. *"Dress Rehearsal Disaster. Details to come."*

Ashley turned to me. "How could Kenny write about the dress rehearsal? It hasn't started yet."

"And how does he know it will be a disaster?" I asked. "Unless—"

We stared at each other. I could tell that Ashley and I were thinking the same thing.

"Unless Kenny knows that something

bad is going to happen—" I started to say.

"—because he's going to *make* something bad happen!" Ashley finished.

"Kenny said his site had been getting tons of hits since the Jingle Bell Jinx started," I pointed out.

"Do you think he's playing all these tricks to have something juicy to report on his site?" Ashley asked.

"I don't know, but I think we should find Kenny—right now! Because if it is him—he's ready to strike again!" I said.

I stared down at the rink. A thin film of water was forming on the top.

"Come on," I called to Ashley. "Kenny's messing up the ice!"

I headed for the ramp. Ashley raced behind me. We sped down to the locker room.

"Mary-Kate, look!" Ashley pointed to the electrical room door. "It's open!"

Ashley and I burst into the room. Kenny

stood by the temperature gauges. He whirled around when he heard us.

His face flushed red. But he grinned as if nothing were going on. "Oh, hi, Mary-Kate. Hi, Ashley. What a surprise to see you guys."

I walked toward him. "We're not surprised to see *you*! We read your latest article—the *Dress Rehearsal Disaster*."

"Oh. Ha-ha. Pretty clever, huh?" He took a step backward. "I can explain."

Ashley folded her arms across her chest. "Really? Then go ahead," she said coolly.

"I—um." He waved toward the temperature gauges. "I heard someone yell that the ice was melting. So I ran down to check the temperature."

"Nice try." I crossed my arms in front of me. "Except no one yelled about the ice melting."

Kenny's face turned a brighter red.

"Oh, and while you're explaining about the ice," Ashley continued, "you can tell us

where you hid Terri's necklace."

"And Lisa's skates," I added. "Come on, Kenny. Admit it. You created the Jingle Bell Jinx so you would have cool news to put on your Web site."

"So you would get lots of hits," Ashley continued.

"What's going on in here?" a voice behind us asked. We turned and found Regina standing in the doorway. The maintenance man was with her.

"Kenny increased the ice temperature," I explained.

Regina's jaw dropped. "Kenny, why would you do such a terrible thing?"

"Kenny has a *lot* of explaining to do," Ashley said. "To everyone."

The maintenance man reached around Kenny and adjusted the temperature of the ice rink. "I'll make an announcement," he told Regina. "Everyone needs to stay off the ice until it hardens."

The maintenance man left the electrical room. Regina turned to face Kenny. "Ashley is right. You have some explaining to do. Let's go."

Kenny gulped loudly.

Regina, Ashley, and I walked Kenny back to the rink. All the skaters were clustered together rinkside. Jake, Patrick, and Mrs. Chan were there, too. Terri had on her elf costume. Lisa wore her lollipop outfit.

Lisa and Terri hurried over to us. "What happened to the ice?" Lisa asked. "Is it the Jingle Bell Jinx again?"

I pointed to Kenny. "*This* is the Jingle Bell Jinx. He is responsible for every bad thing that has happened to you guys."

Kenny swallowed hard. He looked miserable.

"He took your skates, Lisa," Ashley explained. "And your necklace, Terri."

Lisa glared at Kenny. "Terri could have gotten hurt when you switched her tape in

the middle of her routine!"

"And Lisa could have broken her knee when you turned the lights off on her," Terri yelled.

Kenny looked upset. "I didn't mean for anyone to get hurt," he said.

Valerie stepped up beside the sisters. "So *you* were the worm who broke into my locker?"

"Yes." Kenny frowned. "I put the tape in your locker. I planted the tassel and bells, too. So Mary-Kate and Ashley would suspect other people."

"It almost worked," Ashley said.

"I'm really sorry," Kenny said. "I just wanted my Web site to be superpopular."

Regina plucked the video camera from Kenny's arms. "A slushy rink might have been a *real* disaster," she said. "You can stay for the show, but your video days are over."

"Thanks, Regina!" Kenny said. "I'm going

to write an article right now apologizing for everything I've done." He ran off.

Terri hugged Ashley. Lisa hugged me. "Oh, thank you. Thank you so much!" the sisters exclaimed.

Jake clapped his hands. "Now I need to make an announcement." He put his arms around Terri, Lisa, and Valerie. "I am happy to announce that I will now be coaching the *three* most talented skaters in the world!"

Everybody cheered. Ashley and I cheered the loudest. *Excellent!* I thought. Jake wasn't dumping Valerie for Terri and Lisa after all!

Regina stepped forward. "I have an announcement, too. We want to thank Mary-Kate and Ashley for never giving up."

She handed Ashley a silky red costume. It had a flowing skirt and satin bodice. Lisa handed me an emerald green costume. Both costumes had fake fur capes.

"For us?" We gasped.

Regina nodded. "So you can join the show."

My mouth fell open. Ashley's eyes almost popped out of her head.

"Cool! We'll be ice-skating stars!" I exclaimed.

"Well, not exactly *skating* stars." Regina laughed. She pointed to a sleigh that was part of the *Jingle Bells on Ice* set.

"You'll be on the ice," Regina explained. "But you'll be riding in that!"

Everyone laughed. Including Ashley and me. Maybe we wouldn't be skating, but we'd still be in the spotlight!

Then Regina clapped her hands. "Now let's get ready! We have a show to perform!"

All the skaters scattered. Patrick, Jake, and Regina began shouting orders. Ashley and I headed to the locker room to change into our beautiful costumes.

"Performing in the show." I sighed. "What could be more wonderful?"

"There is one thing more wonderful," Ashley said.

I smiled. "What's that?"

Ashley put an arm around my shoulder. "Solving a mystery with a sister you love!"

Hi from both of us,

Ashley and I were thrilled when we were picked to be contestants on our favorite TV game show, _Double Trouble_. But when the show started, it was obvious that someone wanted us to lose—big-time.

If we were going to win, we had to find out who was cheating—on the double!

Want to know more? Slide over to the next page for a sneak peek at our latest case, _The New Adventures of Mary-Kate & Ashley_: _The Case of the Game Show Mystery_.

See you next time!

Mary-Kate Olsen   _Ashley Olsen_

A sneak peek at our next mystery...

The Case Of The
GAME SHOW MYSTERY

"I don't care if you *are* the Trenchcoat Twins," Bobby Branson said. "My twin brother and I are going to beat you!"

With that, Bobby stomped off toward the other side of the room. I shook my head. Ashley and I were thrilled to be on our favorite game show, *Double Trouble*, but the competition was turning out to be tough!

Three other kids were with me backstage. We waited while our twins were on stage, answering questions about us. If our twins answered the questions about us right, we'd get points. If they answered them wrong…we'd get a bucket of green slime dumped on our heads!

"Okay!" called Laurie, the production assistant. "It's time! Everybody on the set!"

We filed out into the bright lights of the stage. I sat down beside Ashley. She gave me a smile and a thumbs-up. "No sweat," she said. "I nailed every question!"

"Okay!" Drew Drewsdale, the host of the show said. "Let's see how well you've done. The first question is, what do you usually have for breakfast? We'll start with Billy and Bobby Branson!"

Across the set Bobby was sitting with his nerdy brother, Billy. Bobby glared at Billy and said, "I *always* have bacon and eggs. *Always*."

"Correct!" Drew said. "That's ten points for the Branson twins."

"Yes!" Bobby said, pumping his fist. Beside him, his brother slumped over. He looked miserable!

What's wrong with him? I wondered.

The host turned to us. "Mary Kate, we asked your sister what you usually have for breakfast. What do you think she said?"

I smiled. This was such an easy one! "I like cereal," I said. "Usually corn flakes."

Ashley grinned at me, but Drew shook his head.

"I'm sorry, Mary-Kate, but Ashley said you like to have a doughnut and chocolate milk for breakfast."

Huh? I looked at Ashley. Ashley was staring at the host, her mouth hanging open in surprise.

"That's not the right answer," the host told us, "which means..."

I heard a click overhead and looked up in time to see—

Sploosh!

Green goop dropped from the ceiling and poured all over Ashley's head.

Ashley turned to me, dripping slime.

"But that's not what I wrote," she whispered. She stood up.

"That's not what I wrote!" she said loudly. "Something's wrong. Someone switched our answers!"

BE A CHARACTER IN A MARY-KATE & ASHLEY BOOK SWEEPSTAKES!

 **The New Adventures of MARY-KATE & ASHLEY™**

 **IT COULD BE YOU!**

COMPLETE THIS ENTRY FORM:

E N T E R

mary-kateandashley.com
America Online Keyword: mary-kateandashley

BE A CHARACTER IN A MARY-KATE & ASHLEY BOOK
Sweepstakes!

Name: _____

Address: _____

City: _____ State: _____ Zip: _____

Phone: _____ Age: _____

Mail to: **BE A CHARACTER IN A MARY-KATE
& ASHLEY BOOK SWEEPSTAKES!**
C/O HarperCollins Publishers
Attention: Children's Marketing Department
10 East 53rd Street
New York, NY 10022

THE NEW ADVENTURES OF MARY-KATE & ASHLEY™
Be a Character in a Mary-Kate & Ashley Book Sweepstakes

OFFICIAL RULES:

1. No purchase necessary.

2. To enter complete the official entry form or hand print your name, address, age, and phone number along with the words "THE NEW ADVENTURES OF MARY-KATE & ASHLEY™ Be a Character in a Mary-Kate & Ashley Book Sweepstakes" on a 3" x 5" card and mail to THE NEW ADVENTURES OF MARY-KATE & ASHLEY Be a Character in a Mary-Kate & Ashley Book Sweepstakes, c/o HarperEntertainment, Attn: Children's Marketing Department, 10 East 53rd Street, New York, NY 10022, postmarked **no later than January 31, 2002**. Enter as often as you wish, but each entry must be mailed separately. One entry per envelope. Partially completed, illegible, or mechanically reproduced entries will not be accepted. Sponsor, as defined below, is not responsible for lost, late, mutilated, illegible, stolen, postage due, incomplete, or misdirected entries. All entries become the property of Dualstar Entertainment Group, Inc., and will not be returned.

3. Sweepstakes open to all legal residents of the United States (excluding Rhode Island), who are between the ages of five and fifteen by January 31, 2002, excluding employees and immediate family members of HarperCollins Publishers Inc. ("HarperCollins"), Parachute Properties and Parachute Press, Inc., and their respective subsidiaries and affiliates, officers, directors, shareholders, employees, agents, attorneys, and other representatives (individually and collectively "Parachute"), Dualstar Entertainment Group, Inc., and its subsidiaries and affiliates, officers, directors, shareholders, employees, agents, attorneys, and other representatives (individually and collectively "Dualstar"), and their respective parent companies, affiliates, subsidiaries, advertising, promotion and fulfillment agencies, and the persons with whom each of the above are domiciled. Offer void where prohibited or restricted by law.

4. Odds of winning depend on the total number of entries received. All prizes will be awarded. Winners will be randomly drawn on or about February 15, 2002, by HarperEntertainment, whose decisions are final. Potential winners will be notified by mail and will be required to sign and return an affidavit of eligibility and release of liability within 14 days of notification. Prizes won by minors will be awarded to parent or legal guardian who must sign and return all required legal documents. By acceptance of their prize, winners consent to the use of their names, photographs, likenesses, and personal information by HarperCollins, Parachute, Dualstar, and for publicity purposes without further compensation except where prohibited.

5. a) One (1) Grand Prize winner will have his or her name included in a Mary-Kate & Ashley book, as a character; and receive an autographed copy of the book in which the winner's name appears. HarperCollins, Parachute, and Dualstar reserve the right to substitute another prize of equal or greater value in the event that the winner is unable to receive the prize for any reason. Approximate retail value: $4.25.

   b) Fifty (50) First Prize winners win an autographed Mary-Kate & Ashley book. Approximate total retail value: $212.50.

6. Only one prize will be awarded per individual, family, or household. Prizes are non-transferable and cannot be sold or redeemed for cash. No cash substitute is available. Any federal, state, or local taxes are the responsibility of the winner. Sponsor may substitute prize of equal or greater value, if necessary, due to availability.

7. Additional terms: By participating, entrants agree a) to the official rules and decisions of the judges, which will be final in all respects; and to waive any claim to ambiguity of the official rules and b) to release, discharge, and hold harmless HarperCollins, Parachute, Dualstar, and their affiliates, subsidiaries, and advertising and promotion agencies from and against any and all liability or damages associated with acceptance, use, or misuse of any prize received in this sweepstakes.

8. Any dispute arising from this Sweepstakes will be determined according to the laws of the State of New York, without reference to its conflict of law principles, and the entrants consent to the personal jurisdiction of the State and Federal courts located in New York County and agree that such courts have exclusive jurisdiction over all such disputes.

9. To obtain the name of the winners, please send your request and a self-addressed stamped envelope (excluding residents of Vermont and Washington) to:

   THE NEW ADVENTURES OF MARY-KATE & ASHLEY™ Be a Character in a Mary-Kate & Ashley Book Sweepstakes
   c/o HarperEntertainment
   10 East 53rd Street, New York, NY 10022
   by March 1, 2002. Sweepstakes sponsor: HarperCollins Publishers, Inc.

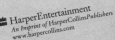

The Ultimate Fan

mary-kat

Don't miss